Fairy

Retold by Barbara Ker Wilson   Illustrated

Cassell, London

Tales of India

The Poor Man's Dream   The Brave Potter
The Four Friends   The Bow of Mithila

by Rene Mackensie

The Poor Man's Dream

This story was told long ago
by a wise Brahmin to three
young Indian princes.
'Once upon a time,' said the
Brahmin, as he sat with the
three princes under the spread-
ing foliage of a banyan tree,
'there lived a man who was
so poor that he had to beg for
food. One day somebody
gave him an earthenware jar
filled with barley meal.
This was a feast for
the beggar, and he
carried the jar back to
his hovel, where he
hung it carefully on a
peg beside his mattress.
Then he lay down
and with his
gaze fixed on the jar,
fell into a day dream.

' "Supposing," he thought,
"there was a famine in
this village, as there was some
years ago, when the river
flooded the fields and destroyed the crops. Then, if I
kept this jar of barley meal, I should be able to
sell it for a hundred rupees. Oh yes, at least a
hundred rupees.

"'And what should I do with this money? Why, I would buy two she-goats, who would give me milk every day. And twice a year they would bear two more she-goats, which I would sell in the market. Soon I should have enough money to buy some cows. Of course, the cows would bear many calves, and these I would sell also. Then I would buy buffaloes—and after buffaloes, mares for breeding horses."

'At this point,' said the wise Brahmin, 'the beggar began to believe that his dream was true. He thought: "Soon the stables of the Rajah himself will be filled with my horses—I can see them in my mind's eye, fine spirited animals with gleaming coats and flaring nostrils!

By this time I shall be the richest man in the village, and all my neighbours will show me respect. With some of my gold I will buy a great house, with mango trees growing beside a cool fountain. Presently a noble lord will come to my house, and offer me his lovely daughter in marriage, together with a large dowry. Her scented hair is as black as a raven's wing, her skin as smooth as lotus petals.

'"Then she will give me a son, whom I shall name Moon-Lord. One day, when Moon-Lord is two or three years old, he will be playing by the stables while I am sitting nearby on the roof, reading a book. He will look up and see the horses, and suddenly run towards them, those spirited animals with their gleaming coats and flaring nostrils. . . . My wife is sitting below me, and in my fear for Moon-Lord I call out to her to run after my son, and stop him going too near the horses. But she does not pay any attention to me.

'"This makes me very angry, and I climb down from the stable roof and beat my wife for her disobedience. I hit her once, twice, three times!"'

'And in his dream,' continued the wise Brahmin, 'the beggar thrashed his arms about as he lay on his mattress. Alas! his hand caught the jar of barley meal that hung on the peg beside him. It fell to the ground and was broken into many pieces. The barley meal was scattered to the four winds, and so were the foolish imaginings of that poor man, who had now lost his next meal.'

And this is the story that was told long ago by the wise Brahmin to the three young Indian princes as they sat under the banyan tree, to teach them that no good can come from wishful thinking.

The Brave Potter

'Where is my poor old beast? Come here, you
miserable animal!'
   The Potter had lost his donkey, and was
searching for it everywhere. Night was not far off, and
with the darkness a storm arose. Rain lashed
down; thunder reverberated around the hills. At last,
through a curtain of falling water, the Potter saw
an animal huddled against the wall of a hut.
'My donkey!' he cried. He went up to the animal,
seized it by one ear, gave it a good beating,
and then carried it home on his back and tied it to a
post outside his house.

In the morning all signs of
the storm had disappeared, and
the hot Indian sun shone
down once more. The Potter's
wife woke up and looked out
of the window.
'Husband! Wake up! There
is a tiger tied to the post
outside the house!' she cried.
The Potter sprang up from
his bed. Sure enough, there was
a large, savage tiger tugging at the
rope that held it to the post.
'And I thought it was my
poor old donkey! I am lucky to
be alive this morning,' said
the Potter, trembling to think of
the way he had beaten the tiger
the night before.

Soon the whole village knew about his amazing exploit, and before long even the Rajah heard of it. He left his palace and visited the village to see the brave man who, alone and unarmed, had captured a savage tiger.

'I need such men as this in my villages,' said the Rajah. He gave the Potter a large house, much land, enough money to fill the village well, and conferred on him the command of ten thousand horse in his army.

The Potter and his wife now wanted for nothing. They lived happily with their new wealth until one day a neighbouring state declared war on the Rajah, and threatened to invade his land with a great army. The Rajah summoned all his princes and asked which of them would lead his soldiers into battle. But none of them would accept the chief command, for they knew that the army was not prepared for war. The Rajah was in despair. Then he remembered a certain Potter who lived in one of his villages.

'Surely,' he thought, 'a man who, alone and unarmed, can capture a savage tiger, must be able to lead my army against the enemy.'

He summoned the Potter to the palace and told
him that he should have the honour of the
chief command of his army. The Potter did not
dare to refuse such an honour, and agreed to lead
the soldiers against the enemy. The Rajah told him
that he would send a horse for him to ride at the
head of the army.

'Alas, wife, what shall I do?' asked the Potter
when he returned home. 'I have never sat on
a horse in my life, and the thought of leading
thousands of men into battle
makes me very nervous
indeed. If only I were a
humble man once again, with
a little house! If only I had
never mistaken that tiger for
my poor old donkey!'

His wife said: 'When the Rajah sends his horse for you, you must say that you want to scout out the enemy's position before leading the army into battle. Then I will help you on to the horse, and that way you will be able to practise riding it.'

In the morning the Rajah's horse arrived, a spirited black charger that tossed its head and rolled its eyes at the Potter. His wife fetched some rope, and when the Potter had managed to scramble on to the horse's back, she tied him into the saddle, passing the rope round his waist and the horse's body, and fixing his feet to the stirrups.

The horse reared and kicked, and then set off in
a full gallop out of the gateway, down
the village street, and across the countryside.
The Potter was terrified and clung to the
animal's mane with both hands.

The enemy was camped in the shadow of the
distant hills; as the horse drew nearer
and nearer to the hills, the Potter grew more
and more frightened. Now the tents of the
enemy were in view; in a desperate effort to
stop the horse, the Potter seized hold
of a young banyan tree as they flew past it. But
all that happened was that the tree was
uprooted; the Potter rode on flourishing the
leafy sapling in his hand.

The enemy sentry saw him coming. 'A giant approaches, riding as fast as the wind on a huge black horse! He tears up the trees of the countryside in his rage!' he cried. 'He is one of the Rajah's army!'

The sentry's cry was repeated from mouth to mouth, and fear made the enemy soldiers exaggerate the report. 'An army of giants approaches, brandishing a forest of trees!' they cried. 'Let us fly for our lives!'

Panic took hold of them; they fled back to their own country on the other side of the hills.

When the Potter galloped into the camp, he found it deserted. Tired out at last, his horse stopped in the midst of the empty tents. The Potter untied the ropes that bound him to the horse, and went into the largest tent. Here he found a letter of surrender left by the enemy commander.

'Well,' said the Potter to himself, 'that was an easy victory. I have put the enemy to flight single-handed!'

He took the letter of surrender and led the horse home. When he got back, he sent the letter to the Rajah. When the Rajah realized that the Potter had put the enemy to flight single-handed, his joy was boundless. He summoned the Potter to his palace, to heap more honours and riches upon him. The Potter set off on foot to the palace, and all along the way, people gathered to praise him.

'See the brave Potter!' they cried. 'He is as modest as he is valiant, for although he commands ten thousand horse, he walks humbly to the palace in his sandals.'

After this, the Potter lived in happiness for the rest of his days—and he never rode a horse again so long as he lived.

The four friends

In the heart of the Indian jungle, where monkeys chatter in the tree-tops and snakes slither through the grass, and where the Hunter comes silently with his net and spear, a little white Goat once found a water-hole. But she was afraid to put down her head to drink.

Now there were three other animals beside the water-hole: a glossy black Raven, perched in a tree, a bright-eyed Rat, safe in his hole in the bank, and a Tortoise who lurked under the water itself.

They all three saw that the little Goat was afraid to drink, and wanted to help her. The Raven looked down and all around from his lofty perch and then called out to the Tortoise: 'There is no enemy in sight. Tell the little Goat that it is safe for her to drink.'

So the Tortoise poked his head above the water and told the Goat what the Raven had said, and she was able to quench her thirst in safety. The bright-eyed Rat crept out from his hole and asked the Goat why she was afraid to drink.

'I have just escaped from the Hunter,' she replied, 'and I feared that he would come up behind me and trap me in his net while I was drinking.'

Then the Tortoise said: 'You see that the Raven, the Rat, and myself are good friends. Why do you not join our company? It is better than living in the jungle alone.'

The Goat gladly agreed to join their company, and for a while the four friends lived happily together.

But one day, the Raven,
the Rat, and the
Tortoise waited in vain beside
the water-hole for the Goat to
join them.
'I fear that something must
have happened to our friend,' said the Raven
sadly.
'Perhaps she has met the Hunter,' said the
Rat.
'We must try to find her,' said the Tortoise.
So the Raven spread his glossy black wings
and flew high above the tree-tops, looking
everywhere for the little Goat. At last he
saw a speck of white far below, and when he
came down to earth, he found the Goat
caught fast in the meshes of the Hunter's net.

'Help me!' cried the Goat. 'The Hunter has left me in his net while he goes off to trap other animals. When he returns, he will kill me.'

The Raven was very sad to see the Goat in this predicament. 'I will fly back to the others and ask them what we can do to help you.'

He returned to the water-hole and told the Rat and the Tortoise what had happened to the Goat.

'Our friend the Rat could gnaw through the meshes of the Hunter's net,' said the Tortoise.

'What a good idea!' said the Rat. 'The Raven can carry me in his bill to the place where the Goat is trapped.'

So the Raven flew off with the Rat dangling from his bill. The little Goat was overjoyed to see them, and the Rat set to work to bite through the meshes of the Hunter's net with his sharp, pointed teeth. He had just bitten through the last mesh, and the Goat was shaking herself free, when who should arrive at that place but the Tortoise.

The other three friends were dismayed to see him there.

'Alas!' cried the Goat. 'Soon the Hunter will return, and how shall you escape him? The Raven can fly up into the tree-tops; the Rat can creep into a hole in the ground; I can run swiftly away. But all you can do is to crawl slowly along. You will never escape him.'

At that moment, the Rat heard with his sharp ears the stealthy tread of the Hunter coming through the jungle. Immediately they all set off from that place as quickly as possible.

The Raven flew to the top of a tall
tree; the Rat crept into a hole; and the
Goat ran away so swiftly that in a
moment she was out of sight. But all the
poor Tortoise could do was to crawl
very, very slowly towards a clump of
tall grasses. . . .

When the Hunter returned, he was
very angry to see the torn net and to find
that the Goat had escaped. He looked
around, and soon spotted the
Tortoise, crawling so very, very slowly
towards the clump of grasses.

'Ha! A plump tortoise is better than nothing,' he cried. He seized the Tortoise, put him in a sack, and strode off.

The Rat, peeping out from his hole, saw what had happened to the Tortoise and told the Raven and the Goat.

'Now we must rescue the Tortoise,' said the Raven. 'How shall we do it?'

'Let me run before the Hunter,' suggested the Goat. 'Then he will drop the sack to pursue me, and the Rat can release our friend the Tortoise.'

The Raven and the Rat agreed to this plan, and the Goat set off. Soon the Hunter caught sight of her as she ran before him. He dropped his sack and began to pursue her. Quickly the Rat ran to the sack and bit through the string that tied it. The Tortoise crawled out thankfully, and hid in the undergrowth. Meanwhile, the Goat led the Hunter cunningly through the jungle, and at last he lost track of her altogether.

He decided that he had had enough hunting for one day, and came back to the place where he had left his sack. 'At least I have a fine plump tortoise here,' he thought to himself. 'That will make good eating to-night!'

When he found the empty sack, he could scarcely believe his eyes. 'Surely this jungle is bewitched!' he said aloud. 'First the swift-footed goat escapes me, then the slow-moving tortoise!'

He suddenly felt afraid, and ran away from that place as fast as he could, with nothing to show for his day's hunting at all.

As for the Raven, the Rat, the Tortoise, and the Goat, they vowed always to help one another in trouble, and in this way they lived in safety in the jungle for many years.

The Bow of Mithila

A thousand times a thousand years ago, Prince Rama lived in India. He was the eldest son of King Dasaratha, whose kingdom lay on the banks of a great river at the foot of the Himalayan mountains. His people were called 'the Children of the Sun' because they were both prosperous and happy. The men were handsome and the women comely; but none were so fair to look upon as Prince Rama. In the royal city of Ayodhya, stately elephants walked the streets, where clear streams flowed, and a beautiful mango grove surrounded the King's palace.

Rama had three brothers. All the brothers were good friends, and there was no jealousy between them, but Rama's inseparable companion was Lakshman, the second son of King Dasaratha. Each of the four princes was clever, and excelled in sports. They could recite the Holy Scripts without fault, and were the best archers and charioteers in the kingdom. They could even take charge of a spirited elephant. Yet Rama surpassed his three brothers in everything. He was indeed, well named 'Rama'—'the greatest joy'.

When Rama was sixteen, he began to attend the royal councils. Even the elders respected the wisdom he showed. His father's people, the Children of the Sun, worshipped their young prince and did him honour in the streets whenever he went forth among them.

One day, an aged man came to the royal palace. He wore the robe of a priestly beggar, and his sandals bore the dust of a long journey. His name was Vishvamitra, and he was the most honoured sage in the land, as full of wisdom as a pomegranate is full of seeds. He had come to King Dasaratha to ask that Rama and Lakshman should return with him to his hermitage for a time, where he would teach them holy lore.

The King gave his consent to this plan, though in his heart he
was sad to see his beloved Rama and Lakshman depart.

So Rama and Lakshman exchanged their princely garments for
the humble garb of huntsmen, and journeyed with Vishvamitra
to his hermitage, where they lived a simple, holy life. Here
Vishvamitra taught Rama the use of sacred weapons so powerful
that no one, be he man or demon, could ever overcome him.

Their sojourn at the hermitage was interrupted by the arrival of a messenger from the Kingdom of Mithila. He told Vishvamitra that King Janaka of Mithila had proclaimed a contest for the hand of his daughter, the Princess Sita, whose beauty was famed in all the Seven Islands of the Earth. Suitors for her hand were flocking to Mithila to take part in the contest.

'Come,' said Vishvamitra to Prince Rama and his brother. 'We too will journey to Mithila. The eldest son of King Dasaratha is no unworthy suitor for the hand of the Princess Sita.'

That same day, they began their journey north, towards the great river Ganges. In four days they reached the Kingdom of Mithila, and made their way to King Janaka's palace. Here they were greeted with the welcoming drink of honey - sweetened water.

'Behold, King Janaka,' said Vishvamitra, 'the two eldest sons of King Dasaratha, who rules over the Children of the Sun. Prince Rama has come as a suitor for the hand of Princess Sita.'

'I have heard of the prosperous and happy Children of the Sun,' replied King Janaka. 'You are welcome.'

Twelve days later, all the suitors entered the arena where the contest was to be held. There were princes and nobles from all the Seven Islands of the Earth. Each one hoped to win the Princess Sita as his bride. The place was crowded with spectators. Musicians played to the waiting throng, the hot Indian sun shone down, and there was excited speculation about who would win the contest. The suitors took their places on a dais. Amongst the other contestants in their gorgeous robes of silk and gold, and their jewelled turbans, Rama was easily distinguishable in his plain huntsman's garments. In spite of his humble clothes, he seemed the most princely of them all.

Trumpets sounded, and King Janaka appeared with Princess Sita by his side. A hush fell upon the crowd as they saw her and marvelled at her beauty. Her hair shone as the raven's wing, her skin was like the lotus petal. Then King Janaka said: 'At Sita's birth I made a vow that her hand should be given in marriage to the youth who could prove his skill with the great bow of the ancient Kings of Mithila. For this purpose we are here now.'

He gave a signal. Into the arena came an eight-wheeled chariot, propelled by five hundred men. The chariot held the mighty bow of Mithila, which had lain unused since the time of the ancient kings, who were men of giant strength. The bow was now strung for the first time in many years.

One by one, the contestants came forward to see if they could draw it. One by one, they failed to do so. No warrior prince from all the Seven Islands of the Earth could even lift the bow from the chariot, let alone draw the string. One by one, they retired with defeat written in their faces.

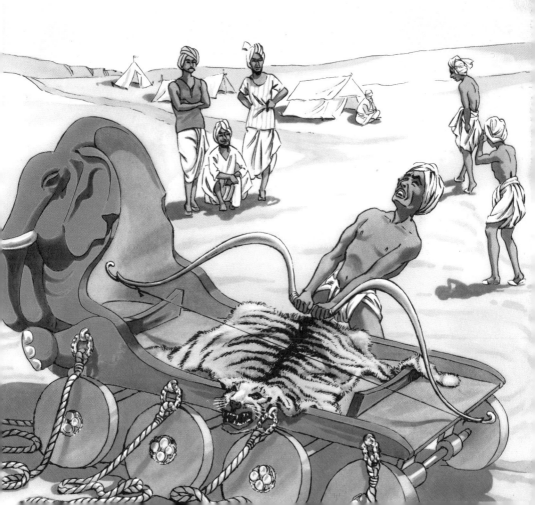

Then Rama stepped forward. As he reached for the great bow, Vishvamitra, in the crowd, called out a blessing upon him. Rama placed his hand upon the bow and with a mighty effort held it aloft. There was a tumultuous shout from the crowd. He pulled on the string; slowly the curved ends of the great bow drew closer together. Suddenly, when the string was pulled to its full extent, the ancient bow snapped in two with a deafening noise. It was as though a thunderbolt had fallen into the arena.

But the cheers and happy shouts of the crowd sounded even louder. With one voice, Rama was acclaimed as the victor of the contest.

King Janaka raised his hand, and the noise died down. He led forth the lovely Princess Sita, and placed her hand in Prince Rama's.

So Rama won his bride, and as long as they lived, he and Sita loved each other dearly. Their life together was filled with adventure, both joyous and sad. The heroic tale of these adventures has been written down in seven famous books, known as the Ramayana, one of the oldest and best-loved sagas of India.

First Published 1960
Reprinted 1967

Made and printed by offset by William Clowes & Sons, Ltd, London and Beccles